Ben Shrimpton, also known as Shrimp, looked carefully at Ms Freeman. After all she was important. She would be teaching his class in September . . .

Suddenly he started listening to what she was saying. That made him sit up. Wow! Ms Freeman was talking, yes, Ms Freeman was talking about a school project in the holidays. School work in the *summer holidays*!

A wonderful story about a very special summer from the author of the hilarious Smarties Prize-winner, *Astrid, the Au Pair From Outer Space.*

Young Corgi books are perfect when you are looking for great books to read on your own. They are full of exciting stories and entertaining pictures and can be tackled with confidence. There are funny books, scary books, spine-tingling stories and mysterious ones. Whatever your interests you'll find something in Young Corgi to suit you: from ponies to football, from families to ghosts. The books are written by some of the most famous and popular of today's children's authors, and by some of the best new talents, too.

Whether you read one chapter a night, or devour the whole book in one sitting, you'll love Young Corgi books. The more you read, the more you'll want to read!

Other Young Corgi books to get your teeth into
ASTRID, THE AU PAIR FROM OUTER SPACE by Emily Smith
LIZZIE ZIPMOUTH by Jacqueline Wilson
BLACK QUEEN by Michael Morpurgo
ANIMAL CRACKERS by Narinder Dhami

THE SHRIMP

For my brother Ronald

And with thanks to Fred Naggs,
of the Natural History Museum

THE SHRIMP
A YOUNG CORGI BOOK: 0 552 547352

PRINTING HISTORY
Young Corgi edition published 2001

1 3 5 7 9 10 8 6 4 2

Set in 16/20pt Bembo Schoolbook by Falcon Oast Graphic Art

Young Corgi Books are published by Transworld Publishers,
61–63 Uxbridge Road, London W5 5SA,
a division of The Random House Group Ltd,
in Australia by Random House Australia (Pty) Ltd,
20 Alfred Street, Milsons Point, Sydney, NSW 2061, Australia,
in New Zealand by Random House New Zealand Ltd,
18 Poland Road, Glenfield, Auckland 10, New Zealand
and in South Africa by Random House (Pty) Ltd,
Endulini, 5a Jubilee Road, Parktown 2193, South Africa

Printed and bound in Great Britain by
Cox & Wyman Ltd, Reading, Berkshire

The Shrimp

Emily Smith

Illustrated by Wendy Smith

YOUNG CORGI

Chapter One

Ben Shrimpton, also known as Shrimp, walked along the beach. He was looking for shells. It had all started when he found an orange shell near his sandcastle. A bit further on he found a pink one. Suddenly he was searching – really searching. He found more shells . . .

different colours . . . different shapes . . .
And, just as he was thinking he really
must turn back, he found it. It was a
new shell, round and delicate. When he
picked it up, it shone with all the
colours of the rainbow.

And something in Ben Shrimpton
went "*Zing!*"

Chapter Two

Ben Shrimpton, also known as Shrimp, looked carefully at Ms Freeman. After all, she was important. She would be teaching his class in September. He hoped she wasn't going to be a shouter. She didn't *look* like a shouter. She had a green stripe through her hair. Somehow he felt that people with green stripy hair wouldn't go in for shouting.

Suddenly he started listening to what she was saying. That made him sit up. Wow! Ms Freeman was talking, yes, Ms Freeman was talking about a school project in the holidays. School work in the *summer holidays*!

Ben glanced round the class. Everyone else seemed aghast too. It was an aghast class, no doubt about it. Some people were frowning. Some were goggling. Some had their mouths open.

Ben waited for someone to say something. He never spoke in class unless he had to. Perhaps that was why people called him Shrimp. That and his size.

It was Kate Askew who spoke up. Or rather burst out. "In the holidays?" she cried. "But we never have homework in the holidays!"

Ms Freeman smiled. "It's not homework," she said.

"Well, it sounds like homework," said Kate.

"A lot like homework," said someone else.

"Well, it's not," said Ms Freeman. "You only have to do it if you want to."

Everyone seemed to cheer up at that.

"And of course," Ms Freeman went on, "you choose your own wildlife project."

Oh, thought Ben, a *wildlife project*. He started chewing his pencil.

"What? Anything?" said someone.

Ms Freeman spread her hands.
"Anything! Birds, flowers, grasses, trees,
insects, pond life . . . anything, just as
long as it's wild."

Ben took the pencil out of his mouth.
And did a most un-Shrimp-like thing.
He asked a question. "Are shells wild?"

A little laugh ran round the class. Ben
felt his face flush. He heard Colin
Oakley whisper, "Way to go, Shrimp!"

Ms Freeman turned her green-striped
head, and looked at Ben. "Shells? Yes,

the seashore is a fascinating habitat."
She gave a thumbs-up sign. "Good
idea!"

Ben put the pencil back into his
mouth. He thought he was going to like
Ms Freeman . . .

Ms Freeman piled some stuff on the
table. "I've brought along some books
and magazines to help you. They've got
some great ideas." She looked round the
class. "Have you ever thought of
comparing spiders' webs, for instance?"

Several people were still grumbling.
"But Ms Freeman—"
"I don't see—"
"How can we—?"
"And next term," Ms Freeman went on, "we'll set everything out for Ray Hatcher."
There was silence.
"The *TV* Ray Hatcher?" said Kate.
Ms Freeman nodded. "He's a friend of mine."

"Wow!" said someone.
"Cool!" said someone.

"Dr Hatcher will be giving a talk on the rainforests." A gleam came into Ms Freeman's eye. "But I'd like *us* to have something to show *him*."

There was silence.

"He's going to judge the projects, and choose the two he likes best. And, then . . ." Ms Freeman paused, a smile on her lips. "He'll take the winners on a field trip. To be filmed as part of his new series."

Someone gasped.

Kate put her hand up. "Would it be OK if you left those books here for a bit?"

Chapter Three

At break everyone seemed to be talking at once.

"Fancy Ms Freeman knowing Ray Hatcher!"

"Fancy Ray Hatcher knowing Ms Freeman!"

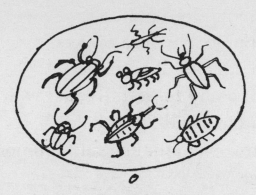

"Remember his scary thing on bugs?"

"Remember? I can't *forget*!"

"Did you see him and that polar bear?"

"We hoped the bear would eat him!"

"I would *so* like to win that competition!"

"I would *so* like to go on a field trip!"

"I would *so* like to be on telly!"

"I might do a project."

"I'll probably do a project."

"I'll *definitely* do a project!"

"I'm going to do this thing with snowdrops," said Spike Riley.

Kate looked thoughtful. "I'm going to do birds."

"Birds?" said Ben.

Kate nodded. "I know a bit about birds."

"Do you go birdwatching?"

"Sure! At first it was just to get to see my dad. And now I'm into them myself."

"It's great, this snowdrop thing," Spike said.

Ben looked at Kate. Suddenly he saw her in a new light.

Ben nodded. "I like birds too. But it's shells I'm really keen on."

"Yeah, right," said Kate. "They don't fly away."

"Well, there's that," said Ben. "But it's also that they're interesting and different and—" He broke off. Someone had come up.

"On about his shells, is he?" said Colin.

Ben nodded.

Colin gave a laugh. "Shells! Very suitable for a Shrimp!"

Ben said nothing. Colin always called him Shrimp (in fact he was the one who started it).

"You need ink for this snowdrop thing," said Spike.

"So what about you, Colin?" asked Kate. "Are you doing a project?"

Colin pursed his lips. "Do you know what I'm going to do?"

They shook their heads.

"Zilch!"

"Oh," said Ben.

"Do you know what zilch is, Shrimp?"

"No," said Ben. Perhaps zilch was a type of seaweed? Or maybe a sort of frog spawn?

"Well, I'll tell you," said Colin. "It means . . . nothing. Zero. Nil."

"I see," said Kate. "So you're not doing a project."

Colin gave a snort. "A wildlife project in the holidays? Give me a break!"

Ben and Kate looked at each other when he was gone.

Kate shrugged. "That is *so* Colin."

Ben nodded. It *was* so Colin.

"Well, no-one's to pinch my snow-drop idea," said Spike.

Kate rounded on him. "You don't get snowdrops in summer, you great nana!"

"Oh," said Spike.

Chapter Four

"Hey, Mum!" said Ben. "I've found a crenulated wentletrap!"

"Hmm?" Mum was sitting on a towel, reading a magazine.

"I found a crenulated wentletrap!"

"Oh dear," said Mum, turning a page.

"It's good, Mum, good!" said Ben. "I haven't got a crenulated wentletrap!"

"Oh," said Mum. "Good, then."

Ben looked at the shell in his hand, and frowned. "At least I think it's a crenulated wentletrap. I'll have to check when I get back."

"Mmmm." Mum pulled her hat further down over her eyes.

It was a hot, hot summer.

Ben was working hard on his shells.

Mum and he weren't taking a proper holiday that year. The car had suddenly needed an expensive new gearbox. And Mum said she thought they had better just have day trips.

Ben was not as disappointed as he

might have been. And whenever Mum asked where he wanted to go, he said the same thing – the beach.

Camber Sands was a long drive away, and sometimes the traffic was terrible.

But it was a wonderful beach, a vast sweep of sand which never got too crowded. It was great for football. And kites. And paddling. And making dams. And swimming. And it was great for finding shells.

Sometimes when they arrived, the tide would be high, and Ben would wait, kicking a football about, until the churning sea slipped away.

Then he knew he was the first to walk along the strand lines. He found the ordinary shells first: tellins and cockles and razor-shells. Then he found more unusual ones, scallops and gapers. Bit by bit he sorted out the best examples. Bit by bit he built up his collection.

He learnt too. He bought a book called *Guide to the Seashore* and took several more out of the library. He studied his seashore guide in the car. It began with plants, and then went up through the animal kingdom, starting

with sponges. (Mum was so surprised to hear that a sponge was an animal she nearly jumped the traffic lights.) Right at the end, after the shells and the shrimps and the fish and the birds, was a page of . . . seals.

Ben loved the pictures of the seals.
They looked so sleek and plump and
friendly. He would really like to see a
seal. But he knew that wasn't very
likely.

As his shell collection
grew, Ben had the
problem of how to store
it. One of his books said
that old chocolate boxes were
good. That sounded promising.
Ben read the bit in the book out to
Mum. When she didn't say anything, he
read it out again. He had just started
reading it for the third time, when Mum

said, "If you think, Benjamin, that I am buying chocolates when I have just bust the zip on my black leather skirt, you, Benjamin, had better think again."

Ben decided to think again. One "Benjamin" was bad enough. Two "Benjamins" was definitely back-off time!

Instead of the chocolate boxes, he made do with shoeboxes and food trays from the supermarket. The tiny shells he kept in a large matchbox, lined with cotton wool.

One afternoon Mum found him cleaning some scallop shells with his toothbrush. "Eeeek!" she exclaimed.

"It's OK, Mum!" said Ben. "It says in my book. It *says* you can clean shells with your toothbrush!"

"Oh, yes?" said Mum. "Does it say *your* toothbrush, or *a* toothbrush?"

Ben checked in his book. "*A* tooth-brush," he admitted.

"Yes," said Mum. "A bit of a difference, that. *A* toothbrush means an *old* toothbrush, not—"

But, before she could really get going, the front-door bell rang.

Chapter Five

It was Ben's aunt, Genna.

"*Surprise!*" she cried, when he opened the door. She held up a load of carrier bags. "Prepare to be amazed! Amazed and delighted! I've come to show off my new clothes!"

She did too. Mum and Ben sat on the sofa and watched her trying everything on.

"What do you think, Ben?" Genna said, striking a pose in a green dress.

Ben gazed at her. "Well, there's not much of it."

Genna threw back her head and laughed. "So like your grandma, darling!"

After everything had been put back in the bags, they had a cup of tea. And it was only then that Genna caught sight of the shells on the table. "Wow, look at these!" she said. "Are these yours, Ben?"

He nodded.

"But they're fantastic! You've laid them out beautifully. And look, you've got some really good ones! However did you find them all?"

Ben gave a shrug.

"Nose in the sand, bottom in the air, that's how he finds them!" said Mum.

Genna laughed.

"And when it's not nose in the sand, it's nose in the shell books,' Mum went on. "You should hear him about boring depths!"

"Boring depths?" said Genna. "What are boring depths?"

"Well, I'm not sure," said Mum. "I tend to drift off at that stage."

They both turned to him. "What are boring depths, Ben?"

Ben gave another shrug. "It's just the depth the different types of shellfish bore down to," he said. "That's all."

"Well, I'm dead impressed!" said Genna. She looked dead impressed too.

"Actually," said Mum, "I'm pretty impressed too . . ."

"Well, you've really inspired me!" said Genna, gazing at Ben's collection.

"When I go to Cornwall with Dave, I'm going to look for shells."

"Going to Cornwall?" said Ben.

"With Dave?" said Mum.

"Yes!" said Genna. "Dave's sister takes this house right on the sea, and we're staying there."

"How lovely!" Mum looked pleased. She approved of Dave.

"Isn't Cornwall rocky?" said Ben.

Genna laughed. "Sure is!"

"Oh!" said Ben.

"What do you mean, 'Oh'?" said Genna.

"Well . . ." He spoke slowly. "It's just that most of my shells are sandy shore ones. And shells on rocky shores are

quite different. You know, limpets and
things." He swallowed. "And I'd really
like . . ."

He broke off.

He realized what
he had done. He had
done a most un-
Shrimp-like thing.
He had more or less
asked if he could go to
Cornwall with them.

Mum looked at him.

Genna looked at him.

Mum looked at Genna.

Genna looked at Mum.

They both looked at him again.

"Hmmm," said Genna slowly. "It *could*
just work too. No promises, mind."

Chapter Six

Genna was right, thought Ben. Cornwall *was* rocky. He was sitting on the pebbly beach a little way from the house, gazing over the sunlit sea. Cornwall was very rocky. It was sandy too in some places, with a coarser sand than at Camber. But it certainly did rocks well. And rock pools.

Ben stirred a pile of limpet shells with his foot, and gave a happy sigh. It had all worked so well, coming to Cornwall with Genna. Dave's family had been kind, and he particularly liked Ellen, Dave's sister. And everyone took an interest in the shells he found.

Ben looked back over the rock pools he had been exploring. It had been a magical morning. He had seen crabs and fish and prawns, and even a starfish. He had seen anemones, some shining like red sweets, others pale and snaky.

Yes, it had been wonderful. But it hadn't been good for his shell collection.

Once his heart had leapt as he saw a beautiful top-shell, but when he tried to pick it up, he got a surprise. It held firm. It was alive. The shell was needed by someone! Sadly he left it.

Three seabirds flew overhead, peeping. Ben looked out over the bay again.

There was a large shape moving across the water. He stared at it. Could it be a seal? *Surely* not . . . He sat up excitedly, and narrowed his eyes at it. But in a second he realized his "seal" was just someone snorkelling. Of course.

Ben settled down again, and dug his
hand in the grey pebbles. Then he heard
a shout. Genna stood at the bottom of
the steps, waving her fishing net. "Come
on!" she said. "Time for tea!"

For some reason, just before he got to
his feet, he looked at the limpet-strewn
pebbles round him. His eye ran over dry
seaweed, an old crisp packet, and some
bits of coloured glass worn smooth by

the sea. And his gaze stopped at a tiny
pale shape. He frowned, and picked it
up. He expected to find it was a pebble
or a bit of broken shell. But it wasn't a
pebble. Or a bit of broken shell.

It was a perfect cowrie shell . . .

Ellen was in the kitchen when they got
back.

She knew at once what his shell was.
"Wow, a cowrie! Did you find that here,
Ben?"

Ben nodded. "Just now, on the pebbly
beach."

"Ooh! Clever you!" Ellen admired
the perfect little shell with its three

brown spots. "Isn't it beautiful?" Then she called her husband. "Rick, come and look!"

Rick came into the kitchen and admired it too. "Hey, well done!"

Genna was looking pleased, but puzzled. "Is a cowrie good, then?"

"It certainly is!" said Ellen.

"I mean, are they rare?"

"Well, I've always heard there are cowries here if you look hard enough. But all these years I've never found one." Ellen gave a little sniff. "Not one!"

Ben looked at her and an awful thought came to him. Ellen had been so welcoming, and always cooked things he liked. And now he had a cowrie, and she hadn't.

He gulped. "Ellen?"

"Yes, Ben?"

He held out his hand. "You can have the cowrie if you like."

"Oh, bless him!" cried Ellen. "*Bless* him!" She looked at Ben with dancing eyes. "I wouldn't *dream* of taking your cowrie, Ben. But it's very kind and generous of you to offer it to me."

Ben smiled back at her. Phew!

On his last day, he checked out the sandy beach after the tide went down, and found a fine dog cockle. Then he grabbed his net and bucket and went rock-pooling. Genna had had enough of rock-pooling by now, but she happily lay on a rock sunbathing and reading her book.

Ben hadn't caught anything new for some time now, but this time he did. Under a ledge in a big rock pool, he netted two little spider crabs. They looked weird, with lots of bits of green seaweed dangling from their legs and bodies. Ben decided to take them back to the house in the bucket and study them.

He found a see-through bowl in the kitchen, and tipped them in. He watched them moving about, and drew a (not very good) picture of one in his notebook.

"Supper?" said Ellen, when she saw the crabs in the bowl. "Only joking!" she added, as she saw the look on Ben's face.

"Hey, Ben!" Genna stuck her head round the door, and threw his swimming trunks at his head. "Come with me and Dave for a last surf!"

He went. He loved holding on to the board as a wave carried him swooshing towards the shore. Even if he did sometimes get a mouthful of water.

When he got back, he suddenly remembered his spider crabs. They were still in the bowl, hardly moving now, and not looking too happy. He knew he ought to return them to the sea.

Ben put them back into his bucket, told Genna what he was doing, and set off. He had decided to go to the sandy beach, which was closest. But then he felt uncertain. He had caught the spider crabs in a rock pool. Shouldn't he return them to a rock pool? They might not survive in the open sea.

He frowned, and turned towards the rock pools. It shouldn't take too much longer. The tide was coming up, he noticed, as he picked his way over the rocks.

He found a nice deep pool, and knelt down at its edge. Then he held his bucket over the water, and gently tipped his crabs in. "Goodbye, spider crabs!" he said. He rose to his feet. And, as he did so, he heard a cry.

Chapter Seven

Ben froze. The bucket swung from his hand. Had he imagined the cry? But no, there it was again. A sort of mewing sound. An *unhappy* mewing sound.

What was it? An animal? A human? A wounded sea-bird?

Ben looked around. He was all alone.

There was no-one else near on the rocks. Suddenly he felt fear. His heart was hammering. He was the Shrimp now, all right. He shouldn't have come so far without telling Genna.

Then he looked back up at the cliff path. He wasn't so alone, after all. There were several walkers, not that far away.

A little girl in a red anorak was running along, with a grown-up trying to catch up. An old couple sat on a bench, looking out to sea. Suddenly he felt better. More like Ben again.

He heard the mewing sound again. And drew a breath.

"Hello?" he said.

There was a scratching, scrabbling sound, and he heard . . . whimpering.

He took a few steps nearer, poised to fly at any moment. Then he heard another whimper, louder, and somehow hollow-sounding. It seemed to be coming from a deep cleft in the rocks about three metres away.

Slowly Ben picked his way over to the cleft. Then, heart thumping, he knelt on the edge, and peered down. Below, at the bottom of a small gully, gazing up at him with dark eyes, was a little dog.

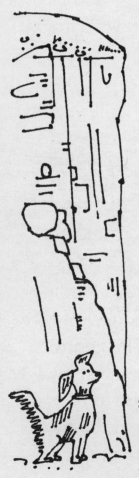

It was a young dog, hardly more than a puppy, with a leather collar round its neck. Ben saw at once what had happened. Somehow it had fallen down, and had been unable to get out, up the steep rock sides.

"It's OK, boy!" he said. "I'll get you out."

Then Ben had a shock. He heard a wave crash, and looked up to see sea-water splashing over the rocks only a couple of metres away.

He hadn't realized how fast the tide had been rising. Within minutes it would be pouring into the gully that had trapped the little dog. He had come just in time.

The puppy whimpered again, as if it knew how close the danger was. Carefully Ben lowered himself into the gully. He made sure he found two good footholds. The puppy watched, shivering. Then Ben bent, scooped it up, and heaved it up on top of the rock.

The puppy stumbled slightly, but then found its feet. It wasn't injured, Ben could see that. With a glance at the sea-spray on a nearby rock, he hauled himself up and out.

As Ben stood on top of the rock again, he felt a rush of triumph.

"Come on, boy!" he said to the puppy. And together they set off towards the steps. It always waited for him, not running on. It clearly thought it best to stick close to its rescuer!

As they climbed the steps, Ben's feeling of triumph was replaced by doubts. What should he do now? What would Ellen say when he turned up with a strange dog?

But he needn't have worried.

Even before he had climbed halfway up, he heard a shout.

"Lottie! Look, someone's found Lottie!"

The little girl in the red anorak came running along the path. Ben could see that her face was red too, from crying. But now her eyes were shining . . .

Chapter Eight

The puppy's family took Ben home in triumph.

Ellen was quite surprised to see a procession come up the path, led by a yapping dog.

The parents told everyone in the house what a hero Ben was. At least three times.

"Losing Lottie would have ruined our holiday," said the dad.

"It would have ruined more than our holiday!" said the mum.

The little girl threw out an arm. "It would have ruined my childhood!"

Everyone laughed. And Lottie tried to jump over the wall, but was caught by Rick, and tied to a gatepost.

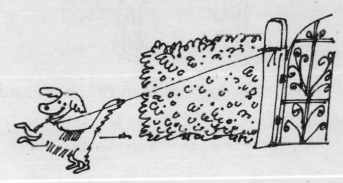

The mum took some photographs of Ben and the puppy with her instant camera, and wrote on the back, "Lottie, rescued by Ben Shrimpton."

Meanwhile the dad went along to the surf shop, and bought Ben a top-of-the-range yellow and green surfboard.

"But I'm going home tomorrow!" said Ben.

"We can have an early-morning surf before we go!" said Genna. "And who knows?" She winked at Dave. "We might be asked again next year!"

"Not a chance!" said Dave. But he winked back.

"Wow!" said Ellen, after they had all gone.

"Nice of them to be so grateful," said Genna.

"So they should have been!" said Ellen.

"But people aren't always grateful when they should be," said Genna.

"That's for sure!" said Rick.

Dave put an arm round Genna. "So pretty, and wise, too."

Genna laughed, and picked up the photo-graph. "I love this picture of you, Ben."

Ben leant towards her, and frowned. "Hmm. Don't I look a bit sort of . . . pleased with myself?"

Genna smiled. "That's what I like about it!"

"You *should* be pleased with yourself!" said Ellen.

"Yes!" Genna ruffled Ben's hair.

"You're my little hero. My star. My starfish!"

★

Ben sat watching the fields flash by the train window. He had socks on for the first time in days.

He glanced at his new surfboard, tucked in the gap behind Genna's seat. That morning it had gone like the wind. *Whoooosh!* Ben smiled at the memory.

But as the train carried him closer and closer to home, Ben's thoughts moved from the past to the future. From the Cornish beach to the classroom.

"Ben?" Genna was looking at him.

"Mmm?"

"What are you thinking about?"

"School."

"Ah." She understood. "It was fun, though, wasn't it, Cornwall?"

"It was great."

Genna blew on her coffee. "You got some good shells."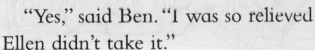

"*And* some!"

Genna smiled. "Like that cowrie."

"Yes," said Ben. "I was so relieved Ellen didn't take it."

Genna winked. "I know. But it was so nice of you to offer it."

She sipped some coffee, getting froth on her nose. "So how did this shell thing really start? Was it because of the competition?"

Ben thought. "No, I was interested before then. But the competition made

me . . . concentrate. Do my research." He
took out his seashore guide, looking
battered and curled after so much use.

Genna nodded at it. "Have you found
everything in there, then?"

"No way! But I've made an OK
collection."

"An OK collection?" Genna repeated,
laughing. "Oh, Ben! Your collection's a
cracker, you know it is!"

"Well . . ."

"And I bet you win that competition!"
Ben shook his head. "Doubt it."

"You doubt it?" cried Genna. "After spending all summer working on your shells? Well, if there's any fairness in this world . . ." Genna paused and looked thoughtful. "Mind you, I'm sometimes not sure there *is* much." Suddenly she grinned, and pinched his knee. "But at least there are *aunts*!"

For some time they were silent. Then Genna nodded again at his guide book. "So, what haven't you got then?"

Ben frowned. "It's not something to collect. More something to see."

"Really?"

"And it's not a shell either."

The train was beginning to slow.

"Well, what is it, then?" said Genna, getting to her feet.

"A seal."

And Genna turned, and stared at him . . .

Chapter Nine

Ben laid his shell collection carefully on the table in Ms Freeman's room.

"Wow, Ben!" said Kate. "You've been working hard!"

"Yeah," said Ben.

"And look at your labels. I didn't know you could write so neat!"

"No," said Ben.

"I love those sweet little teeny shells. They're ditsy!"

"If you say so," said Ben.

"Well done, Shrimp!" said Raj.

Now Ms Freeman came over. "Hey, look at those!" she said. "Well done!" She gazed at the table. "In fact there's been a lot of good work."

Ben looked at the table too.

There were all sorts of things. There were collections of shells, collections of flowers, collections of leaves. There were bark-rubbings, an ant-farm crawling

with ants, and some experiments using jam jars. Someone, surely Melissa, had done a huge project on ponies, complete with horse tack and rosettes. (Melissa wouldn't let the fact that ponies weren't exactly wildlife put *her* off!) And there were a sheaf of neat bird drawings that Ben knew at once were Kate's.

"Those bark-rubbings were really difficult," grumbled Raj. "I kept making holes in the paper."

Suddenly Ms Freeman pointed a finger. "Whose is that?"

They all looked.

There, at the end of the table, was a pot with a dead, very dead, plant in it.

No-one knew anything about it, but suddenly Kate said, "I wonder if *Spike* has anything to do with it?"

Spike did have something to do with it. "Yes," he said. "It's my wildlife project."

"But . . . what sort of project?" asked
Ms Freeman.

"It's an interesting experiment," said
Spike.

"Oh, yes?" said Ms Freeman. "What
sort of interesting experiment?"

"Well," Spike explained, "it shows what
happens when you go away on holiday
and leave a plant without water."

He looked quite hurt when everyone
burst out laughing.

"OK, Spike!" Ms Freeman was smiling
too. "But you'll have to write it up prop-
erly. Plant name, dates, everything."

Not everyone had done a project. One of these was Colin, who went round telling anyone who would listen about the villa his family had taken in Italy. "It had this amazing pool, and a maid and a cook and everything," Ben heard him tell Raj at break.

"Gosh!" said Raj, impressed. "A villa with a cook."

"And I learnt lots of Italian. I can now ask for twelve different sorts of ice-cream."

"Twelve! That's a lot!" Raj paused. "So you didn't do a wildlife project?"

Colin shook his head. "Couldn't. Just didn't have the time." He curled his lip. "Anyway, I reckon wildlife projects are for anoraks!"

Raj looked surprised. "Anoraks?"

"Yeah," said Colin. "Anoraks."

When Colin had gone off, Raj came over to Ben and Kate and Spike. He was frowning. "What are anoraks?" he asked.

"They're sort of jackets," explained Spike. "And sometimes they've got a sort of fluffy bit on the hood, and toggle things on them, and—"

"Be quiet, Spike," said Kate. "You're not explaining at all." She looked at Raj. "What Colin was saying, in his Colin way," she said, "was that people who do wildlife projects are, well . . uncool."

There was silence.

"Well, are they?" said Raj. "Are they uncool?'

Kate thought a bit. "Well, look at it this way, Raj. If being interested in wildlife is uncool, then Ray Hatcher and Ms Freeman and you and me and my dad and almost all the other people in our class are uncool. And Colin is cool. Or thinks he is!" She spread her hands. "So take your pick!"

"Come to think of it," said Spike. "I don't think anoraks have toggles at all."

Chapter Ten

The class settled down quickly.
Everyone got used to their new room,
their new books, their new teacher.

Ben was pleased to find that he had
been right about Ms Freeman. She was
not a shouter. She got a bit ratty sometimes, like the time when all the scissors
went missing. But she was not a shouter.

On Friday, she told the class that Ray Hatcher would be coming the following week. Suddenly everyone was excited again.

What would Ray Hatcher look like in real life? Would he like their projects? *Who* was going to go on that field trip? And would they really be on television?

Colin listened to the talk in silence. And then he wandered over to the projects table. His eyes swept over the work displayed and suddenly stopped at Ben's shells. "Hmmm," he said, half to himself. "Shells . . ."

The following Monday Ben walked into the classroom and got the shock of his life.

There was a crowd round the projects table. "They're fantastic, Colin!" he heard Melissa say. He squeezed through the people and stood staring in amazement. There, right in the middle of the table, was a treasury of shells!

They were shells which took your breath away: huge shells, delicate shells, pearly shells, spotted shells, shells with spirals and horns and wings and teeth. They mostly (Ben knew from his books) came from warm blue distant seas. They had names like conch, Venus comb, nautilus . . . And they were all displayed on a smart wooden unit.

Ben kept staring. In one part of his mind he was feasting his eyes on the glorious shells. In another he was furiously working out what had happened. Two days ago Colin hadn't even got a project! He *said* he hadn't! And now . . .

Suddenly Ben clicked. That was it! Now he knew what Colin had done. He'd just gone to a shell shop, or somewhere, and bought the most beautiful shells he could see. Colin hadn't done a wildlife project at all. He was a cheat!

"Wow . . ." breathed someone beside Ben. "Those are amazing."

"Hey, Col!" someone else said behind him. "You're bound to win with those."

"Well, I don't know." Colin sounded smug. "But I must stand a good chance."

Ben was hardly listening. He could only gaze. Suddenly he thought of his own collection. He glanced over.

There it was, arranged in its shoeboxes and plastic trays. And somehow, compared to this exotic display of Colin's, it looked . . . childish. Tatty and childish. He turned back to Colin's shells. They were shimmering now. And he realized he was very close to tears . . .

Chapter Eleven

"He's smaller than he looks on telly," said Kate.

"No, bigger," said Raj. "I reckon he's bigger."

"He's not who I was expecting at all," said Spike. "I was expecting the other one."

"Oh, *Spike!*" said Kate.

It was break-time on the day of Ray Hatcher's visit. Dr Hatcher had given a talk to the class on the rainforest. And now he and Ms Freeman were looking at the wildlife projects.

"He was amazing about the rainforest, wasn't he?" said Raj.

"I never knew about those lakes in the rainforest," said Ben.

"I'd love to see some of those birds," sighed Kate.

"To think of all those animals becoming extinct!" said Raj.

There was silence. "We *must* save the rainforests!" said Spike.

Everyone looked at each other.

"Spike," said Kate.

"Yes?" said Spike.

"For once, Spike, you are absolutely right!"

Ben gave a sigh. "I think he's wonderful."

"Who?" said Raj.

"Dr Hatcher!"

"He certainly knows his stuff," agreed Kate.

"It's not just that," said Ben. "He's . . . *wonderful*. He's not all out for himself like some famous people. He really does care about wildlife."

"How can you tell?" said Raj.

Ben thought, then shrugged. "I just can."

Suddenly there was silence again, as everyone looked towards the classroom.

"I wonder how they're getting on," said Kate.

"He's probably decided by now," said Raj.

"Ooo-er!" said Spike.

"I wonder who it is," said Raj.

"Bet I know one of them," said Kate.

"Yeah," said Spike.

There was a thoughtful silence.

"I'd love to go on that field trip," said Raj.

"Me, too," said Kate.

"Me too," said Spike.

Me too, thought Ben.

He had always liked the idea of the wildlife field trip.

But now he had heard Dr Hatcher talk, and seen the fire in his eyes, he wanted it more than anything else in the world . . .

Chapter Twelve

"There's some wonderful work on that table." Ray Hatcher twinkled round at everyone. Everyone looked back at Ray Hatcher. "I have really enjoyed looking at some of the projects. It's so good to see bright young people take an interest in wildlife."

He walked slowly over to the projects table, and stood there, gazing down at it. There was absolute quiet in the classroom. Then suddenly he looked up again, and smiled. "There's so much good work, it has been very difficult, but . . . I finally decided on these." He leant forward, and picked up Kate's project. "These beautiful bird drawings."

Ms Freeman turned towards her, and smiled. "Well done, Kate."

So she'd done it! Kate had done it!

And she would go on the field trip! Ben glanced over. Kate looked pink with pleasure.

Dr Hatcher held up a few of the drawings. And he and Kate talked about thrushes and blackbirds, and their different calls.

Then there was a pause. And then Dr Hatcher said, "I'm sorry, but I don't think this can really be called a wildlife project."

Ben raised his head. Dr Hatcher was pointing at Colin's shells!

"They are magnificent, but I suspect they were bought from a shop or collector." His eye ran over the display. "I'm not saying you should never buy shells, but I think some of these may have been taken live from the sea."

They all looked at him blankly.

"That means the animal was killed so its shell could be sold."

85

A murmur went round the class.
"Sometimes people cut the molluscs
out, sometimes they boil them, and
sometimes they 'hang' them. The shell is
hung up, so that the poor animal just
gets longer and longer, drooping down,
until it dies." Dr Hatcher made a face.
"Not nice."

Ben looked round at his friends' faces.
They clearly thought it was "not nice"
either. In fact that was putting it mildly.

Ben glanced over at Colin. It was now his turn to look pink. And suddenly he felt a strange feeling. He actually felt *sorry* for Colin.

"However . . .!" Suddenly the twinkle was back in Dr Hatcher's eyes. "There is a wonderful collection of shells here. A collection into which someone has clearly put a lot of work, and, I suspect, a lot of love. And that person is my other winner."

"Ben!" Ms Freeman smiled at him. "Could you come up, please?"

Up? He had to go *up*? But he was Shrimp. Going up was not his sort of thing. There was no help for it. Spike grinned and rolled his eyes, as Ben stumbled forwards. He stood by the table, hanging his head.

"Did you collect all these yourself?" asked Dr Hatcher.

There was a pause.

And in those seconds something happened. Or rather Ben realized that something had happened. He had changed over the summer. He had gone out and taught himself about the seashore. He had rescued a dog. He had made a shell collection singled out by a famous naturalist. *He wasn't Shrimp any more.*

Ben lifted his head. "Yes, I collected these," he said. "Every single one."

Dr Hatcher smiled. "Well, you've done well, there are some nice specimens here." He picked up a razor-shell, showed it to the class, then turned to Ben. "What's this?"

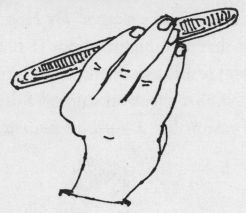

Ben grinned. That was easy. "It's a razor shell."

Dr Hatcher nodded. "And do you know why it's called a razor?"

"Yes," said Ben promptly. "Because it looks like an old-fashioned razor, the sort people used to shave with."

"Absolutely right."

Dr Hatcher put down the razor, and turned to Ben with a sudden grin. "Come on!" he said. "Show us your favourite! Show us your favourite shell!"

For a second or two Ben's hand hovered over the Cornish cowrie. And then he darted and chose.

"Ah, yes, a saddle oyster." Dr Hatcher took the shell gently, turning it so the mother-of-pearl caught the light. "A lovely one too." He looked Ben in the eye. "Tell us about it."

So Ben did. He told them saddle oysters were bi-valves, and had two halves, and showed the hole in the shell by which it stuck to rocks.

And when he had finished explaining all that, Dr Hatcher said, "But you haven't told us something."

Ben looked at him. "What?"

"You haven't told us why this is your favourite shell."

Ben smiled. And then he told them about the day he had found the saddle oyster. The day he had picked it up, gleaming with all the colours of the rainbow. The day something in him had gone "*Zing!*"

Chapter Thirteen

Ben sat in the boat, as it swung against the quay. He was wearing an orange life jacket.

"'Take this!" Kate flung him her rucksack. He grabbed it, and she settled down on the seat beside him. She looked out at the grey sea. "Any idea, yet?" she said. "Do you know what we're looking for?"

Ben shook his head. "Uh-uh."

"Me neither," said Kate.

"Could be seabirds?" said Ben thoughtfully. "Or some sort of fish."

"Octopus?" said Kate.

"In Norfolk? I think not," said Ben dryly.

Kate looked at him. "Hmm," she said. "You're different nowadays, you know.

You'd never have talked like that before."

"Wouldn't I?" said Ben.

Kate shook her head. "I mean, I can't see anyone calling you Shrimp now."

Ben laughed. "Prawn, then?"

"More like Lobster!" said Kate.

Ben made his hand into a claw and started nipping her arm, and Kate pulled her sleeve away, laughing. "Ow, stop it!"

Suddenly Kate pointed at a black-and-white bird, flying past. "Look, an oystercatcher!" She grinned happily. "I love oystercatchers! They're so . . . black and white!"

"And red," added Ben. "Their beaks are red."

Kate stuck her nose in the air. "We birders say 'bills'."

Paul the cameraman climbed carefully into the boat, then took out his camera.

"Ooh!" said Kate.

Ben grinned. "Hope he doesn't drop it in the sea."

A second cameraman was standing by another boat, which was moored further up along the jetty. Ms Freeman was already sitting in that one. She leant forward and shouted at them. "Hey, don't get cold, put your anoraks on!"

"Make us!" Kate called back naughtily.

Ms Freeman shook her fist in pretend anger. "If I have to tell your parents you've got colds, you'll be for it!"

"No way am I wearing an anorak over a life jacket," Kate said. "It'd look dead stupid!"

Ben nodded. "And we wouldn't show up orange if we fell in."

"I don't intend to fall in," said Kate, looking at the dark water with a shiver. "Too cold!"

"Cast off!" Suddenly Dr Hatcher
threw Ben the rope, jumped in, and
started the outboard motor with a sharp
tug. They were away!

Dr Hatcher settled back, and looked at them with his keen blue eyes. "Well, here we go," he said. "This is the first part of our field trip." He smiled. "And I don't need to tell you to keep your eyes open."

Ben nodded. He still felt a bit shy with Ray Hatcher. But he was happy just to be with him . . .

Paul trained the camera on Dr Hatcher as he spoke above the roar of the motor. "Well, here we are on the North Norfolk coast, steering out to sea in the good boat *Mary Jane*. And why?

Well, that I can't tell you right now, because this trip is what you might call a Magical Mystery Tour for two young naturalists here with me, Ben Shrimpton and Kate Askew." By this time Paul had turned and focused the camera on their faces, and Dr Hatcher went on talking about them.

The boat chugged evenly out to sea
for about two miles. The other boat
caught them up, and moved smoothly
alongside. "I hope we're going to be
lucky," Dr Hatcher was saying to the
camera. "We should be seeing one of
our mystery animals fairly soon now.
But of course, where wild animals are
concerned, you can never . . ."

Ben gazed out of his side of the boat. Nothing. He looked out of Kate's side of the boat. Nothing. He looked up in the sky. But all he could see were a few gulls flapping towards land. The boat chugged on, starting to round the sand-bank.

And just then he saw it. It was only a few yards away. Looking at him from between the waves was . . . a head, a round grey head with soft brown eyes, and a curious friendly expression.

Ben knew at once what it was, he had gazed at the picture so often in his seashore guide. He nearly fell out of the boat with excitement. "It's a seal!" he shouted. "Oh, oh, it's a seal!"

And then another head popped up. And another. And another. And Ben tasted salt-spray on his lips, and a thrill in his heart.

Chapter Fourteen

"I told you your collection was a cracker!" said Genna.

"Hmm, they do look good," Ben admitted, as the camera panned slowly over his shells.

"And this was the collection that won Ben Shrimpton his place on the field trip," Ray Hatcher was saying in a voice-over.

"I can see a crenulated wentletrap!" shouted Mum, pointing excitedly.

"And there's your cowrie from Cornwall," said Dave, sounding pleased.

The four of them were sitting in Ben's front room, watching the television.

Suddenly the picture changed to two boats at a quay.

"Ah," said Mum. "Now we're getting to the field trip."

Then the boats were heading out to
sea, and the camera closed in on Dr
Hatcher, steering the boat and talking
over the sound of the outboard motor.

"What's he really like?" asked Genna.

"Sssh!" said Mum. "I want to hear
every word."

"He's *wonderful*!" whispered Ben.

Genna nodded, looking at the screen.
"Well, he makes a good programme,"
she said. "I like the idea of a mystery
wildlife tour."

Now the camera focused on Ben and Kate, looking pale and wind-swept in their life jackets.

"I can see Ben!" shouted Mum, pointing excitedly.

"Oh, Ben!" cried Genna. "You do look sweet!"

"*Sweet?*" said Ben.

"I mean, um . . . cool!" said Genna hastily.

They all looked at the screen.

"And sort of confident . . ." said Mum thoughtfully.

"Yes." Genna turned to him. "You know what you've done, don't you, Ben Shrimpton?"

"No," said Ben. "What have I done?"

Genna smiled. "You have really come out of your shell."

And Ben looked at her. And grinned . . .

THE END

ASTRID, THE AU PAIR FROM OUTER SPACE
Emily Smith

Imagine being looked after by an alien from outer space. . .

When Harry's mum says they're getting an 'au pair' from another country, he's not quite sure what to expect. When Astrid, who lives on a planet 500 light years away, decides to work as an 'au pair' on Earth, she's not quite sure what to expect.

What Harry definitely doesn't expect is a girl whose suitcase moves on its own, whose hair sticks out like a dandelion clock and who doesn't know what football is.

And Astrid is very surprised to find that Harry's family has a special gadget for opening tins and that his little brother Fred isn't a girl!

A hilarious story of family fun!

0 552 54616X
YOUNG CORGI
Books to get your teeth into

ANIMAL CRACKERS
Narinder Dhami

"Mr Jackson," Sanjay said faintly. "You've turned into a polar bear."

When Sanjay gets a bump on the head from the school bully, he wakes up to find that everyone in the playground has turned into an animal. The headmaster's a polar bear and Sanjay's best friend is a sheepdog. Even the ambulance that comes to rescue him is driven by a gorilla.

Seeing his schoolmates in a new light gives Sanjay a cunning idea, in this crackingly funny story.

0 552 546267

YOUNG CORGI
Books to get your teeth into